Legends
of
Irish Witches and Fairies

PATRICK KENNEDY

THE MERCIER PRESS

THE MERCIER PRESS
4 Bridge Street, Cork

© The Mercier Press, 1976
This edition 1991

ISBN 978 1 78117 922 2

PUBLISHER'S NOTE

The stories in this book are taken from Patrick Kennedy's works *Legendary Fictions of the Irish Celts*, *The Fireside Stories of Ireland* and *The Banks of the Boro* published in Dublin between 1866-1870.

Transferred to Digital Print-on-Demand in 2024

CONTENTS

1 : THE LONG SPOON

The devil and the hearth-money collector for Bantry set out one summer morning to decide a bet they made the night before over a jug of punch. They wanted to see which would have the best load at sunset, and neither was to pick up anything that wasn't offered with the goodwill of the giver. They passed by a house, and they heard the poor *vanithee* cry out to her lazy daughter, 'O musha, the devil take you for a lazy *sthronshuch* of a girl! do you intend to get up today?' 'Oh, oh!' says the tax-man, 'there is a lob for you, Nick.' '*Ovoch!*' says the other, 'it wasn't from her heart she said it; we must pass on.' The next cabin they were passing, the woman was on the bawn-ditch crying out to her husband, who was mending one of his brogues inside: 'Oh, tattheration to you, Mick! you never rung them pigs, and there they are in the potato drills rootin' away; the devil run to Lusk with them!' 'Another windfall for you,' says the man of the inkhorn, but the old thief only shook his horns and wagged his tail. So they went on, and ever so many prizes offered to the black fellow without him taking one. Here it was a gorsoon playing marvels when he should be using his clappers in the corn-field, and there it was a lazy drone of a servant asleep with his face to the sod, when he ought to be weeding. No one thought of offering the hearth-money man even a drink of buttermilk, and at last the sun was within half a foot of the edge of Cooliagh. They were just then passing thro'

Monamolin, and a poor woman that was straining her supper in a skeeoge outside her cabin door, seeing the two standing at the bawn-gate, bawled out, 'Oh, here's the hearth-money man, the devil run away wid 'im!' 'Got a bite at last,' says Nick. 'Oh, no, no! It wasn't from her heart she said it,' says the collector. 'Indeed an' it was from the very foundation stone of her heart it came. No help for misfortunes; in with you,' says he, opening the mouth of his big black bag; and whether the devil was ever after seen taking the same walk or not, no one ever laid eyes on his fellow-traveller again.

2: THE PROPHET BEFORE HIS TIME

About a hundred years ago lived Mr Diarmuid
K., a strong gentleman-farmer of this family. His
place was not far from *Slieve Buie* (Yellow Hill).
He was much addicted to the study of astrology,
and the occult works of Cornelius Agrippa. When
his only son was about a month old, one of his servant boys ran into the parlour one day to tell him
a circumstance that had greatly astonished himself:
'Oh, master,' said he, 'the black cow was just while
ago under the old thorn tree in the meadow, and all
the rest of the field was in the sunshine. I was
going over to see what was the matter, when what
should I see but a big seagull flying into the fog,
and making ever so much noise with his wings. For
fear he'd pick out the poor beast's eyes I ran over,
but just as I got to the edge of the fog it all cleared
as if there was some magic in it, and Blacky was
walking away on the other side.' 'Oh, ho!' said the
master, 'what I have been long wishing for has happened at last. Now, Pat, attend to what I say.
Watch that cow close; and when she calves, be sure
to bring me some of the first beestings, and I'll give
you more money than you have ever seen at once
in your own possession.'

The boy did his duty, such as it was. He brought
the first beestings to his master, and received 10*l.*
for his pains and Mr K. ordering the child to be
brought to him, made it take a spoonful or two of
this first milk of the black cow. When the child

7

began to speak intelligibly, the master of the house called all the family together one day, and charged them as they valued his favour, or dreaded his resentment, never to ask his son a question till he was full fourteen years of age. 'The questions, I mean,' said he, 'are such as he could not answer without being a prophet. He is gifted with a spirit of prophecy, and when he reaches his fifteenth birthday, you will be at liberty to get all the information you please from him, concerning anything that is passing anywhere in any part of the world at the moment, or to ask about things lost or stolen, or your own future destiny. But attend to what I say. If you ask a question of him before he is full fourteen years of age, something terrible shall happen to him and you; take timely warning.'

The boy had a wonderful capacity for science and language, but seldom spoke to those about him. He was very amiable, however, and every one anxious for some favour from his father always got him to be their spokesman. Strange to say, he reached to within a few days of the fatal time without being asked an improper question by any one.

He would occasionally when in company start and begin to talk of what was passing at the moment in the town of Wexford, or the cities of Dublin or London, as if the people about him were aware of these matters as well as himself. Finding, however, by their looks and expressions of surprise, that they had not the same faculty, he began to grow very silent and reserved.

About this time a granddaughter of the famous Blacky was about to calve; and Mr K., who set a great value on the breed, recommended her particularly to the care of a young servant boy, a favourite of his. While he was looking after her and some others in a pasture near the house, a young girl to whom he was under promise of marriage was passing by chance along the path that bordered the fence. He asked her to stop, but 'she was in a hurry to the big house.' Stop she did, however, and full twenty minutes passed unmarked while they stood and conversed on very interesting nullities.

At the end of the twenty minutes he gave a sudden start, and examined the different groups of cattle with his eyes, but no Blacky was to be seen. He searched, and his betrothed assisted, but in vain, and the poor girl burst out a crying for the blame he would be sure to get through her folly. She went forward at last on her message to the big house, and passing by the kitchen garden, whom should she see, looking at the operations of the bees, but the young master. Let her not be blamed too much! She forgot everything but her lover's mishap; and so, after making her curtsey, she cried out across the hedge, 'Ah! Master Anthony, alanna, do you know where the black cow has hid herself?' 'Black cow!' said he, 'she is lying dead in the byre.' At that moment his eyes opened wide as if about to start from his head, an expression of terror took possession of his features, he gave one wild cry, fell powerless on his face, and when his wretched father came running to the spot, on hearing of the circumstance, he found an idiot in the place of his fine intelligent son.

3: THE BEWITCHED CHURN

Near the townland of Scarawalsh there lived an old woman of bad repute with her neighbours. She was seen, one May eve, skimming a well that lay in a neighbouring farm, and when that was done, she went into the adjoining meadow, and skimmed the dew off the grass. One person said he heard her muttering, 'Come all to me, and none to he.' In a day or two, the owner of the farm, coming in from the fields about noon, found the family still at the churn, and no sign of butter. He was a little frightened, and looked here and there, and, at last, spied a bit of stale butter fastened to the mantel beam of the open fire-place.

'Oh, you may as well stop,' said he, 'look what's there!' 'Oh, the witch's butter,' said one of the girls, 'cut it off the mantlepiece.' 'No use,' said another, 'It must be a charmed knife, or nothing. Go and consult the fairy man, in the old ruined house at ——. If he doesn't advise you, nobody can.' The master of the house took the advice, and, when they had milk enough for another churning, this is what they did.

They twisted twigs of the mountain ash round their cows' necks, they made a big fire, and thrust into it the sock and coulter of the plough; they fastened the ash twigs round the churn, and connected them to the chain of the plough-irons; shut door and windows, so that they could not be opened from without; and merrily began the churning.

Just as the plough-irons were becoming red-hot, someone tried the latch of the door, and immediately they saw the face of the witch outside the window. 'What do you want, good woman?' 'The seed of the fire, and I want to help you at the churning. I heard what happened to you, and I'm rather lucky.' Here she roared out; for the burning plough-irons were scorching her inside. 'What ails you, poor woman?' 'Oh I have a terrible colic! Let me into the fire for mercy's sake, and give me a warm drink.' 'Oh, musha, but it's ourselves are sorry for you; but we could not open door or window now for St Mogue himself; for 'fraid the witch 'ud come in and cut our quicken gads, or pull out the plough-irons, or even touch the churn-staff. She got a bit of butter out of the fresh churning the other day; and took a sod out of our fire; and till she brings back the butter and the sod we must labour away. Have patience, poor woman; when we see a sign of the butter we'll open the door for you, and give you such a warm tumbler of punch, with caraways in it, as would bring you back from death's door. Put more turf on, and keep the irons at red heat.' Another roar ensued, and the she ejaculated, 'Oh, purshuin' to all hard-hearted naygurs, that 'ud see a fellow-creature dying in misery outside of their door! Sure, I was coming to yous with relief, and this is the sort of relief you'd give me. Throw up the window a bit, and take those things I made out for yous. Throw the bit of butter you'll find in this sheet of white paper into the churn, and this sod of turf into the fire, and cut away the bit of butter on the mantel beam with this

11

knife, and give it back to me, till I return it to the knowledgeable woman I begged it from for yous.'

The direction being followed, the butter began to appear in heaps in the churn. There was great joy and huzzaing, and they even opened the door to show hospitality to the old rogue. But she departed in rage, giving them her blessing in these words, 'I won't take bit nor sup for yez. Yez have thrated me like a Hussian or a Cromwellian, and not like an honest neighbour, and so I lave my curse, and the curse of Cromwell on yez all!'

4: THE GHOSTS AND THE GAME OF FOOTBALL

There was once a poor widow woman's son that was going to look for service, and one winter's evening he came to a strong farmer's house, and this house was very near and old castle. 'God save all here,' says he, when he got inside the door. 'God save you kindly,' says the farmer. 'Come to the fire.' 'Could you give me a night's lodgings?' says the boy. 'That we will, and welcome, if you will only sleep in a comfortable room in the old castle above there; and you must have a fire and candle-light, and whatever you like to drink; and if you're alive in the morning I'll give you ten guineas.' 'Sure I'll be 'live enough if you send no one to kill me.' 'I'll send no one to kill you, you may depend. The place is haunted ever since my father died, and three or four people that slept in the same room were found dead next morning. If you can banish the spirits I'll give you a good farm and my daughter, so that you like one another well enough to be married.' 'Never say't twice. I've a middling safe conscience, and don't fear any evil spirit that ever smelled of brimstone.'

Well and good, the boy got his supper, and then they went up with him to the old castle, and show-ed him into a large kitchen, with a roaring fire in the grate, and a table, with a bottle and glass, and tumbler on it, and the kettle ready on the hob. They bade him goodnight and God speed, and went off as if they didn't think their heels were half swift enough.

'Well,' says he to himself, 'if there's any danger, this prayerbook will be usefuller than either the glass or tumbler.' So he knelt down and read a good many prayers, and then sat by the fire, and waited to see what would happen. In about a quarter of an hour, he heard something bumping along the floor overhead till it came to a hole in the ceiling. There it stopped, and cried out, 'I'll fall, I'll fall.' 'Fall away,' says Jack, and down came a pair of legs on the kitchen floor. They walked to one end of the room, and there they stood, and Jack's hair had like to stand upright on his head along with them. Then another crackling and whacking came to the hole, and the same words passed between the thing above and Jack, and down came a man's body and went and stood upon the legs. Then comes the head and shoulders, till the whole man, with buckles in his shoes and knee-breeches, and a big flapped waistcoat and a three-cocked hat, was standing in one corner of the room. Not to take up your time for nothing, two more men, more old-fashioned dressed than the first, were soon standing in two other corners. Jack was a little cowed at first; but found his courage growing stronger every moment, and what would you have of it, the three old gentlemen began to kick a *puckeen* as fast as they could, the man in the three-cocked hat playing again' the other two.

'Fair play is bonny play,' says Jack, as bold as he could; but the terror was on him, and the words came out as if he was frightened in his sleep; 'So I'll help you, sir.' Well and good, he joined in the sport, and kicked away till his shirt was wringing wet, savin' your presence, and the ball flying from one end of the room to the other like thunder, and still not a word exchanged. At last the day began to break, and poor Jack was dead beat, and he thought, by the way the three ghosts began to look at himself and themselves, that they wished him to speak.

'So,' says he, 'Gentlemen, as the sport is nearly over, and I done my best to please you, would you tell a body what is the reason for yous coming here night after night, and how could I give you rest, if it is rest you want?' 'Them is the wisest words,' says the ghost with the three-cocked hat, 'you ever said in your life. Some of those that came before you found courage enough to take a part in our game, but no one had *misnach* enough to speak to us. I am the father of the good man of next house, that man in the left corner is my father, and the man on my right is my grandfather. From father to son we were too fond of money. We lent it at ten times the honest interest it was worth, we never paid a debt we could get over, and almost starved our tenants and labourers.

'Here,' says he, lugging a large drawer out of the wall, 'here is the gold and notes that we put together, and we were not honestly entitled to the one half of it; and here,' says he, opening another drawer, 'are bills and memorandums that'll show who were wronged, and who are entitled to get a great deal paid back to them. Tell my son to saddle two of his best horses for himself and yourself, and keep riding day and night, till every man and woman we ever wronged be rightified. When that is done, come here again some night; and if you don't hear or see anything, we'll be at rest, and you may marry my grand-daughter as soon as you please.'

Just as he said these words, Jack could see the wall through his body, and when he winked to clear his sight, the kitchen was empty as a noggin turned upside down. At that very moment the farmer and his daughter lifted the latch, and both fell on their knees when they saw Jack alive. He soon told them everything that happened, and for three days and nights did the farmer and himself ride about, till there wasn't a single wronged person left without being paid to the last farthing.

The next night Jack spent in the kitchen he fell asleep before he was after sitting a quarter of an hour at the fire, and in his sleep he thought he saw three white birds flying up to heaven from the steeple of the next church.

Jack got the daughter for his wife, and they lived comfortably in the old castle, and if he was tempted to hoard up gold, or keep for a minute a guinea or a shilling from the man that earned it through the nose, he bethought him of the ghosts and the game of football.

5: THE CAT OF THE CARMAN'S STAGE

A carman was leaving Bunclody one morning for Dublin, when what should he see but a neighbour's cat galloping along the side of the road, and crying out every moment, 'Tell Moll Browne, Tom Dunne is dead, tell Moll Browne, Tom Dunne is dead.' At last he got tired of this ditty, and took up a stone and flung it at the cat, bidding himself, and Tom Browne, and Moll Dunne, to go to Halifax, and not to be botherin' him. When he got to Luke Byrne's in Francis Street, where all the Wicklow and Wexford carmen used to stop he was taking a pot of beer in the taproom, and began to tell the quare thing that happened on the road. There was a comfortable-looking gray cat sitting by the fire, and the moment he mentioned what the Bunclody cat was saying, she cried out, 'That's my husband! That's my husband!' She made only one leap out through the door, and no one ever saw her at Luke Byrne's again.

6: CAUTH MORRISY LOOKING FOR SERVICE

Well, neighbours, when I was a *thuckeen* about fifteen years of age, and it was time to be doing something for myself, I set off one fine day in spring along the yalla highroad; and if anybody axed me where I was goin' I'd make a joke about it, and say I was goin' out of Ireland to live in the Roer. Well, I travelled all day, and dickens a bit o' me was the nearer to get a service; and when the dark hour came I got a lodging in a little house by the side of the road, where they were drying flax over a roaring turf fire. I'll never belie the *vanithee* her goodness. She gave me a good quarter of well-baked barley bread, with butter on it, and made me sit on the big griddle over the ash-pit in the corner; but what would you have of it? I held the bread to the fire to melt the butter, and bedad the butter fell on the lighted turf, and there it blazed up like vengeance, and set the flax alight, and the flax set the tatch afire, and maybe they didn't get a fright. 'Oh, musha, vanithee,' says they, 'wasn't it the divel bewitched you to let that *omadhán* of a girl burn us out of the house and home this way? Be off, you torment, and purshuin' to you!' Well, if they didn't hunt me out and throw potsticks, and tongses, and sods o' fire after me, lave it till again; and I run, and I run, till I run head foremost into a cabin by the side of the road.

The woman o' the house was sitting at the fire,

18

and she got frightened to see me run in that way. 'Oh, musha, ma'am,' says I, 'will you give me shelter?' and so I up and told her my misfortunes. 'Poor colleen,' says she, 'my husband is out, and if he catches a stranger here he'll go mad and break things. But I'll let you get up on the hurdle over the room, and for your life don't budge.' 'I won't,' says I, 'and thank you, ma'am.' Well, I was hardly in bed when her crooked disciple of a man kem in with a sheep on his back he was after stealing. 'Is everything ready?' says he. 'It is,' says she. So with that he skinned the sheep, and popped a piece down into the biling pot, and went out and hid the skin, and buried the rest o' the mate in a hole in the flure, and covered it with the griddle, and covered the griddle again with some o' the clay he removed from the flure. Well, when he made his supper on the mutton he says to his wife, 'I hope no one got lodging while I was away,' 'Arrah, who'd get it?' says she. 'That's not the answer I want,' says he. 'Who did you give shelter to?' 'Och, it was only to a little slip of a girl that's as fast as the knocker of Newgate since eleven o'clock, on the hurdle.' 'Molly,' says he, 'I'll hang for you some day, so I will. But first and foremost I'll put the stranger out o' pain.' When I hear him talk I slip down, and was out o' the door in a jiffy; but he was as stiff as I was stout, and he fling the hatchet after me, and cut off a piece of my heel. 'Them is the tricks of a clown,' says I to myself, and I making away at the ling of my life. But as luck would have it, I got shelter in another cabin, where a nice old man was sitting over the fire, reading a book. 'What's the matter, poor girl?' says he, and I up and told him what happened me. 'Never fear,' says he, 'the man o' the mutton won't follow you here. I suppose you'd like your supper.' Well, sure enough, the fright and the run, and the cut heel, and that, made me hungry, and I didn't refuse a good plate o' stirabout.

'Colleen,' says the man, 'I can't go to sleep early in the night, maybe you'd tell a body a story.' 'Musha, an the dickens a story meself has,' says I. 'That's bad,' says he, 'the fire is getting low: take that booran out to the clamp, and bring in the full of it of turf.' 'I will, sir,' says I. But when I took a turf out of the end of the clamp five hundred sods tumbled down on me, head and pluck, and I thought the breath was squeezed out of me. 'If that's the way,' says I, 'let the old gentleman himself come out, and bring in his firing.'

So I went in, and had like to faint when I came to the fire. 'What ails you, little girl?' says he. 'The clamp that fell on me,' says I. 'Oh, but it's meself that's sorry,' says he. 'Did you think of e'er another story while you were at the clamp?' 'Indeed an I didn't.' 'Well, it can't be helped. I suppose you're tired. Take that rushlight into the barn, but don't set it on fire. You'll find plenty of dry straw for a bed, and come into your breakfast early.' Well, I bade him goodnight, and when I came into the barn, sure enough, there was no scarcity of straw. I said my prayers, but the first bundle I took out of the heap I thought all the straw in the barn was down on my poor bones. 'O *vuya, vuya,* Cauth,' says I to myself, 'if your poor father and mother knew the state you're in, wouldn't they have the heartscald.' But I crept out and sat down on a bundle, and began to cry.

I wasn't after cryin' a second *dhrass* when I heard steps outside the door, and I hid myself again under the straw, leaving a little peep-hole. In came three as ugly-looking fellows as you'd find in a kish o' brogues, with a coffin on their shoulders. They wondered at the candle, but they said nothing till they put the coffin down, and began to play cards on it with the dirtiest deck I ever seen before or since. Well, they cheated, and scolded, and whacked one another, and in two minutes they were as great as pickpockets again.

At last says one, 'It's time to be goin', lift the corpse.' 'It's easy say lift,' says another. 'You two have the front, and I must bear up all the hind part —I won't put a hand to it.' 'Won't you?' says the others, 'sure there's little Cauth Morrisy under the straw to help you.' 'Oh, Lord, gentlemen, I'm not in it at all,' says myself; but it was all no use. I had to get under one corner, and there we trudged on in the dark, through knocs, and ploughed fields, and bogs, till I thought the life would leave me.

At last at the flight of the night, one of them says, 'Stop here, and Cauth Morrisy will mind the corpse till we come back. Cauth, if you let anything happen to the honest man inside you'll sup sorrow — mind what I say.' So they left me, and lonesome and frightened I was, you may depend.

But wasn't I frightened in earnest when I heard the corpse's knuckles tapping inside o' the lid. 'O, sir, honey,' says I, 'what's troubling you?' 'It's air I want,' says he, 'lift up the lid a little.' I lifted up a corner. 'That won't do,' says he, 'I'm stifling. Throw off the lid, body and bones.' I did so, and

21

there was a wicked-looking old fellow inside, with a beard on him a week old. 'Thankee, ma'am,' says he, 'I think I'll be easier for that. This is a lonesome place them thieves left me in. Would you please to join me in a game of spoil-five?' 'Oh, musha, sir,' says I, 'isn't it thinking of making your soul you ought to be?' 'I don't want your advice,' says he, 'maybe I haven't a soul at all. There's the cards. I deal — you cut.'

Well, I was so afeared that I took a hand with him; but the dirty divel, he done nothing the whole time but cursin', and swearin', and cheatin'. At last say I to myself, 'I can't be safe in such company.' So I threw down the cards, though I was within three of the game, and walked off. 'Come back and finish the game, Cauth Morrisy,' says he, shouting out, 'or I'll make it the bad game for you.' But I didn't let on to hear him, and walked away. 'Won't you came back, Cauth?' says he; 'then here goes.' Well, the life had like to leave me, for I heard him tearing after me in his coffin, every bounce it gave striking terror into my heart. I ran, and I bawled, and he bawling after me, and the coffin smashing against the stones. At last, where did I find myself but at the old gentleman's door, and if I didn't spring in and fasten the bolt, leave it till again.

'Ah, is that you, my little colleen? I thought you were asleep. Maybe you have a story for me now.' 'Indeed an' I have, sir,' says I, an' I told him all that happen me since I saw him last. 'You suffered a good deal,' says he. 'If you told me that story before, all your trouble i'd be spared to you.' 'But how could I tell it, sir,' says I, 'before it happened?' 'That's true,' says he, and he began to scratch his wig. I was getting drowsy, and I didn't remember anything more till I woke next morning in the dry gripe of the ditch with a *bochyeen*, under my head. So—

There was a tree at the end of the house,
and it was bending, bending,
And my story is ending, ending.

7: BLACK STAIRS ON FIRE

On the top of the hill of *Cnoc-na-Cro'* (Gallows Hill) in Bantry, just in full view of the White Mountain, Cahir Rua's Den, and Black Stairs, there lived a poor widow, with a grandchild, about fifteen years old. It was All-Hallows Eve, and the two were about going to bed when they heard four taps at the door, and a screaming voice crying out. 'Where are you, feet-water?' and the feet-water answered, 'Here in the tub.' 'Where are you, band of the spinning wheel?' and it answered, 'Here, fast round the rim, as if it was spinning.' 'Besom, where are you?' 'Here, with my handle in the ash-pit.' 'Turf-coal, where are you?' 'Here, blazing over the ashes.' Then the voice screamed louder, 'Feet-water, wheel-band, besom, and turf-coal, let us in, let us in:' and they all made to the door.

Open it flew, and in rushed frightful old hags, wicked, shameless young ones, and the old boy himself, with red horns and a green tail. They began to tear and tatter round the house, and to curse and swear, and roar and bawl, and say such things as almost made the poor women sink through the hearthstone. They had strength enough however to make the sign of the cross, and call on the Holy Trinity, and then all the witches and their master yowled with pain. After a little the girl strove to creep over to the holy water croft that was hanging at the bed's head, but the whole bilin' of the wicked creatures kep' in a crowd between her and

24

it. The poor grandmother fell in a faint, but the little girl kep' her senses.

The old fellow made a frightful music for the rest, stretching out his nose and playing the horriblest noise on it you every heard, just as if it was a German flute. 'Oh!' says the poor child, 'if Granny should die or lose her senses what'll I do? and if they can stay till cock-crow, she'll never see another day.' So after about half an hour, when the hullabullo was worse than ever, she stole out without being noticed or stopped, and then she gave a great scream, and ran in, and shouted, 'Granny, granny! come out, come out, Black Stairs is a-fire!' Out pelted both the devil and the witches, some by the window, some by the door; and the moment the last of them was out, she clapped the handle of the besom where the door-bolt ought to be, turned the the button in the window, spilled the feet-water into the channel under the door, loosed the band of the spinning-wheel, and raked up the blazing coal under the ashes.

Well, the poor woman was now come to herself, and both heard the most frightful roar out in the bawn, where all the company were standing very *lewd* of themselves for being so easily taken in. The noise fell immediately, and the same voice was heard. 'Feet-water, let me in.' 'I can't,' says feet-water; 'I am here under your feet,' 'Wheel-band, let me in.' 'I can't—I am lying loose on the wheel-seat.' 'Besom, let me in.' 'I can't—I am put here to bolt the door.' 'Turf-coal, let me in.' 'I can't—my head is under the *greeshach*.' 'Then let yourselves and them that owns you have our curse for ever and a day.' The poor women were now on their knees, and cared little for their curses. But every Holy Eve during their lives they threw the water out as soon as their feet were washed, unbanded the wheel, swept up the house, and covered the big coal to have the seed of the fire next morning.

8: THE WITCHES' EXCURSION

Shemus Rua was awakened from his sleep one night by noises in his kitchen. Stealing to the door, he saw half a dozen old women, sitting round the fire, jesting, and laughing, his own old housekeeper, Madge, quite frisky and gay, helping her sister crones to cheering glasses of punch. He began to admire the impudence and imprudence of Madge, displayed in the invitation and the riot, but recollected on the instant her officiousness in urging him to take a comfortable posset, which she had brought to his bedside just before he fell asleep. Had he drunk it he would have been just now deaf to the witches' glee. He heard and saw them drink his health in such a mocking style as nearly to tempt him to charge them, besom in hand, but he restrained himself. The jug being emptied, one of them cried out, 'It is time to be gone,' and at the same moment, putting on a red cap, she added—

By yarrow and rue,
And my red cap too,
   Hie over to England.

Making use of a twig which she held in her hand as a steed, she gracefully soared up the chimney, and was rapidly followed by the rest. But when it came to the housekeeper's turn, Shemus interposed. 'By your leave, ma'am!' said he, snatching twig and cap. 'Ah, you desateful ould crocodile! If I find you here on my return, there'll be wigs on the green.'

> By yarrow and rue,
> And my red cap too,
> Hie over to England.

The words were not out of his mouth when he was soaring above the ridge-pole, and swiftly ploughing the air. He was careful to speak no word (being somewhat conversant in witch lore), as the result would be a tumble, and the immediate return of the expedition. In a very short time they had crossed the Wicklow hills, the Irish Sea, and the Welsh mountains, and were charging at whirlwind speed the halldoor of a castle. Shemus, only for the company in which he found himself, would have cried out for pardon, expecting to be mummy against the hard oak door in a moment, but all bewildered he found himself passing through the keyhole, along a passage, down a flight of steps, and through a cellar door keyhole, before he could form any clear idea of his situation.

Waking to the full consciousness of his position, he found himself sitting on a stillion, plenty of lights glimmering round, and he and his companions, with full tumblers of frothing wine in hand, hobnobbing and drinking healths as jovially and recklessly as if the liquor was honestly come by, and they were sitting in Shemus's own kitchen. The red birredh had assimilated Shemus's nature for the time being to that of his unholy companions. The heady liquors soon got in their brains, and a period of unconsciousness succeeded the ecstasy, the headache, the turning round the barrels, and the 'scattered sight' of poor Shemus. He woke up under the impression of being roughly seized, and shaken and

28

dragged upstairs, and subjected to a disagreeable examination by the lord of the castle, in his state parlour. There was much derision and laughter among the whole company, gentle and simple, on hearing Shemus's explanation; and as the thing occurred in the dark ages, the unlucky Leinsterman was sentenced to be hung as soon as the gallows could be prepared for the occasion.

The poor Hibernian was in the cart proceeding on his last journey, with a label upon his back, and another on his breast, announcing him as the remorseless villain who for the last month had been draining casks in my lord's vaults every night. He was striving to say a prayer, when he was surprised to hear himself addressed by his name, and in his native tongue, by an old woman in the crowd. 'Ach, Shemus, alanna! is it going to die you are in a strange place, without your *cappeen dearg!*' These words infused hope and courage into the victim's heart. He turned to the lord, and humbly asked leave to die in his red cap, which he supposed had dropped from his head in vault. A servant was sent for the head-piece, and Shemus felt lively hope warming his heart while placing it on his head. On the platform he was graciously allowed to address the spectators, which he proceeded to do in the usual formula composed for the benefit of flying stationers: 'Good people all, a warning take by me;' but when he had finished the line, 'My parents rared me tenderly,' he unexpectedly added, 'By yarrow and rue,' etc. and the disappointed spectators saw him shoot up obliquely through the air in in the style of a skyrocket that had missed its aim. It is said that the lord took the circumstance much

29

to heart, and never afterwards hung a man for twenty-four hours after his offence.

9: THE ENCHANTMENT OF
GEARÓID IARLA

In old times in Ireland there was a great man of the Fitzgeralds. The name of him was Gerald, but the Irish, that always had a great liking for the family, called him *Gearóid Iarla*—Earl Gerald. He had a great castle or rath at Mullaghmast, and whenever the English government were striving to put some wrong on the country, he was always the man that stood up for it. Along with being a great leader in a fight, and very skilful at all weapons, he was deep in the black art, and could change himself into whatever shape he pleased. His lady knew that he had this power, and often asked him to let her into some of his secrets, but he never would gratify her.

She wanted particularly to see him in some strange shape, but he put her off and off on one pretence or other. But she wouldn't be a woman if she hadn't perseverence, and so at last he let her know that if she took the least fright while he'd be out of his normal form, he would never recover till many generations of men would be under the mould. 'Oh!' She wouldn't be a fit wife for Gearóid Iarla if she could be easily frightened. Let him but gratify her in this whim, and he'd see what a hero she was!' So one beautiful summer evening, as they were sitting in their grand drawing room, he turned his face away from her, and muttered some words, and while you'd wink he was clever and clean out of sight, and a lovely goldfinch was flying about the room.

The lady, as courageous as she thought herself, was a little startled, but she held her own pretty well, especially when he came and perched on her shoulder, and shook his wings, and put his little beak to her lips, and whistled the delightfullest tune you ever heard. Well, he flew in circles round the room, and played hide and go seek with his lady, and flew out into the garden, and flew back again, and lay down in her lap as if he was asleep, and jumped up again.

Well, when the thing had lasted long enough to satisfy both, he took one more flight into the open air, but by my word he was soon on his return. He flew right into his lady's bosom, and the next moment a fierce hawk was after him. The wife gave one loud scream, though there was no need, for the wild bird came in like an arrow and struck against a table with such force that the life was dashed out of him. She turned her eyes from his quivering body to where she saw the goldfinch an instant before, but neither goldfinch nor Earl Gerald did she ever lay eyes on again.

Once every seven years the Earl rides round the Curragh of Kildare on a steed, whose silver shoes were half an inch thick the time he disappeared, and when these shoes are worn as thin as a cat's ear, he will be restored to the society of living men, fight a great battle with the English, and reign King of Ireland for two score years.

Himself and his warriors are now sleeping in a long cavern under the rath of Mullaghmast. There is a table running along through the middle of the cave. The Earl is sitting at the head, and his troopers down along in complete armour both sides of the table, and their heads resting on it. Their horses, saddled and bridled, are standing behind their masters in their stalls at each side; and when the day comes, the miller's son that's to be born with six fingers on each hand will blow his trumpet, and the horses will stamp and whinny, and the knights awake and mount their steeds, and go forth to battle.

Some night that happens once in every seven years, while the Earl is riding around the Curragh, the entrance may be seen by anyone chancing to pass by. About a hundred years ago, a horse-dealer that was late abroad and a little drunk, saw the lighted cavern, and went in. The lights, and the stillness, and the sight of the men in armour cowed him a good deal, and he became sober. His hands began to tremble, and he let fall a bridle on the pavement. The sound of the bit echoed through the long cave, and one of the warriors that was next to him lifted his head a little, and said in a deep hoarse voice, 'Is it time yet?' He had the wit to say, 'Not yet, but soon will,' and the heavy helmet sunk down on the table. The horse-dealer made the best of his way out, and I never heard of any other one getting the same opportunity.

10: THE MISFORTUNES OF BARRETT THE PIPER

Barrett the Piper, you see, lost his skill, and was advised to go the the Black North to recover it (Barrett was a Munster man). Well, he took his little boy with him and they walked and they walked till the dark came, and they went into a cabin by the roadside to look for lodging. 'God save all here!' says they. 'Save you kindly!' says the man of the house, but he left out the Holy Name. 'How are you, Jack Barrett?' 'Musha, pure and hearty, sir; many thanks for the asking but how did you know me?' 'Och, I knew you before you were weaned. Sit down and make yourself at home; here you stay till morning.' Well, faith, they got a good supper of potatoes and milk, and a good bed of straw was made for them by the wall up near the fire, and they lay down quite comfortable to get a good sleep. But some bad thoughts came over Jack Barrett in the dead of the night, and he got up and went out of the bed, and it's in the fields he found himself, and a couple of mad dogs running after him. There was a big tree near him with ever so many crows' nests in the top, and he run and climbed up in it from the dogs, and if he missed the dogs he found the crows, and didn't they fall on him to tear his eyes out! He bawled, and he roared, and the man of the house came into the kitchen, and stirred the fire, and there was Jack Barrett on the hen-roost, and the cocks and hens cackling

34

about him. 'Musha, the sorra's on you for a Jack Barrett! How did you get up there among the fowl?' 'The goodness knows; it's not their company I want. Will you help me down, honest man?'

Well, he got into bed again, and if he did he was not long there when a bad thought came into his head and up he got. He was going into the next room, when where did he find himself but by the bank of a big river, and the same two dogs tearing along like vengeance to make gibbets of him. There was a tree there, and its boughs were out over the river. Up climbs Jack, and up after him with the dogs; and to get out of their clutches he scrambled out on a long bough. The dogs were soon feeling after him, and he going our farther and farther, till he was afraid it would break. At last he felt it cracking, and he gave a roar out of him that you'd hear a mile off, and the man of the house came into the kitchen, and stirred the fire, and there was Jack sthraddle-leg on the pot-rack. 'Musha, Jack, but you're the devil's quare youth at your time o' life to be makin' a horse of my pot-rack. Come down, you *onshuch*, and go to bed.'

Well, the third time, where did the divel guide him but to a bed in the next room, and when he flopped into it, he let such a yowl out of him that you'd think it was heaven and earth was coming together. 'What's in the win' now, Jack?' says the man o' the house. 'Oh, it's in the pains of labour I am,' says the unfortunate piper. 'Will we send for the midwife for you?' says the other. 'Oh, the curse o' Cromwell on yourself an' the midwife!' says the poor man, 'it wasn't God had a hand in us the hour we darkened your door. Oh, tattheration

35

to you, you ould thief! won't you give us some aise?' 'Father honey,' says the boy, 'it's *pishrogues* is an you. A drop of holy water will do you more good nor the master o' the house, God bless him!' 'I'll tear you limb from limb,' says the ould villain when he heard the Holy Name, 'if you say that again.' 'Well, anyhow,' says the boy, 'make the sign of the cross on yourself, father, and say the Lord's Prayer.' The poor ould piper did so, and at the blessed words and the sign, his pains left him. There was no sight of the man of the house on the spot then; maybe he was in the lower room.

When the piper and his son woke next morning, they were lying in the dry moat of an ould rath that lay by the high road.

11: THE WOMAN IN WHITE

Pat Gill, of the county of Kildare, was driving towards Dublin, with a load of country produce. He had made a comfortable seat for himself on the car, and had plenty of hay about him and under him. He was pleasantly employed thinking of nothing in particular, dozing and giving an eye to the proceedings of his beast. He was between the mill of Baltracy and the cross-roads of Borraheen, when he was startled by the appearance of a woman dressed in long white clothes, crossing the fence and advancing into the road. She came up to the horse, and walked on with him, close by his neck. The driver chucked the beast's head to the opposite side, for fear he should tread on her feet or long robes, but she still kept as close to him as before, and sometimes he thought he could see the lower part of the horse's fore leg through her dress. The matter had now become very serious. He could not keep his eyes of the apparition, and he felt his whole frame covered with a cold perspiration. He became bewildered, and could not determine either on going on or stopping. So, the horse, finding matters left to himself jogged on apparently unconscious of his fellow-wayfarer. The centre of the cross-roads of Borraheen is or was occupied by a patch of green turf; and when they came to its edge, the white figure stood still, while a portion of the shaft of the car on that side seemed to pass through her. Gill, observing this, drew the beast at once to the other side, crying in a voice made tremulous by terror. 'By your leave, ma'am!' On went horse and car, the edges of the load preventing him from seeing the white form. Having advanced two or three yards, he looked back, fearing to see a mangled body on the road behind him, but he saw, instead, the white appearance standing in the centre of the plot of grass, her hand seeming to shade her eyes, as she looked earnestly after him. Terrified as he was, he never turned his gaze till a bend in the road cut off the view.

12: THE GHOST OF GRAIGUE

A lady in the neighbourhood of that old town, much celebrated for her charities, died, and great sorrow was felt for her loss. Many masses were celebrated, and many prayers offered up for the repose of her soul, and there was a moral certainty of her salvation among her acquaintance. One evening, after the family had retired to rest, a servant girl in the house, a great favourite with her late mistress, was sitting beside the fire, enjoying the dreamy comfort of a hard-worked person after the day's fatigues, and just before the utter forgetfulness of sleep. Her mind was wandering to her late loved mistress, when she was startled by a sensation in her instep, as if it were trodden upon. 'Bad manners to you for a dog,' said she, suspecting the 'coley' of the house to be the offender. But to her great terror, when she looked down and round the hearth, she could see no living thing. 'Who's that?' she cried out, with the teeth chattering in her head. 'It is I,' was the answer, and the dead lady became visible to her. 'Oh, mistress darling!' said she, 'What is disturbing you, and can I do anything for you?' 'You can do a little,' said the spirit, 'and that is the reason I have appeared to you. Every day and every hour some one of my friends is lamenting me, and speaking of my goodness, and that is tormenting me in the other world. All my charities were done only for the pleasure of having myself spoken well of, and they are now prolonging my punishment. The only real good I ever did was to give, once, half-a-crown to a poor scholar that was studying to be a priest, and charging him to say nothing about it. That was the only good act that followed me into the other world. And now you must tell my husband and my children to speak well of my past life no more, or I will haunt you night after night.' The appearance, the next moment, was no longer there, and the poor girl fainted the moment it vanished. When she recovered, she hastened into her settle-bed, and covered herself up, head and all, and cried and sobbed till morning.

Everyone wondered the next day to see such a troubled countenance. But she went through her business one way or other, though she could not make up her mind to tell her master what she had seen and heard. She dreaded the quiet hour of rest; and well she might, for the displeased lady visited her again at the same hour, and reproached her for her neglect. Three times she endured the dread visits before she made the required revelation.

13: DROOCHAN'S GHOST

A townland north of Mount Leinster is infested by the above-named evil spirit. Within a few years, sundry people returning from a cross-roads' dance, on a Sunday evening, just as night had set in, were greatly terrified. Their road lay along the side of a tolerably steep hill, and as they were coming on, and chatting, they heard the most dreadful cries above them, and a noise as of rocks tumbling down directly to crush them. They ran away at their best speed, and still heard the unearthly yells higher up, and the dreadful sounds, as if half the rocks and loose stones on the heights were sweeping down, crossing the road behind them, and plunging head-long into the stream at the bottom of the hill. Terror and dismay ruled the neighbourhood that night, and for a week longer, when the fright of the Sabbath-breakers was turned to anger and shame. The wag of the next village had carried an empty cask to the summit of the hill, supplied the inside with some stones, fastened the end securely, and just as the gossipers came below, he let slip the engine.

Droochan, the bugbear of the district, had been a man of evil life, and consequently entitled after his death, to annoy all peaceable subjects that had the ill luck to live in his neighbourhood.

A small family in that blighted vicinity were taking their evening meal in their little parlour, when they were alarmed by their servant-girl

41

rushing across the hall from the kitchen, and crying out, 'Oh, masther, masther, Droochan's ghost! He's in the kitchen.' After fifteen minutes spent in exclamations, hasty questions, confused answers, and researches, the following dialogue took place: 'What shape did he appear to you in?' 'Oh, I didn't see him at all!' 'Who saw him?' 'The cats.' 'How do you know?' 'Ah, sure there wasn't a breath stirrin', when them two craythurs cocked their ears, stood up on their hind legs, wud their eyes stanin' in their heads, and sparred at one another with their hands—I mean their fore paws. Then they let a yowl, as if heaven and earth was coming together, and run off into the coal shed. And what ghost could they be seeing only Droochan's?'

14: THE ENCHANTED CAT OF BANTRY

Long ago, after the English first came to Ireland, there were continual fights and skirmmages between themselves (their great strength was down in the baronies of Forth and Bargy), and the people in the upper part of the country, who would have no rulers except the old royal blood of Leinster, the O'Kavanaghs. Parties from each side would drive away cattle from their enemy, and kill the owners if they persisted. A little *bodach* of the English side that lived off towards Ballinvegga came in the dead of the night with a boy of his to a lonesome house somewhere near the Glounthaan, killed the poor owner, and some of his family, and drove away all the cattle that were in the place, and that was only a cow and a sheep. But mind, when they were getting home they found themselves pursued, and had no way to save their lives but by breaking into a chapel. I don't know whether it was the one at Rathgarogue or Temple Udigan.

When the crowd went by, and they were relieved of their fright, they began to feel hungry. So they killed the sheep, and were roasting a quarter of it at a fire they made out of old coffin boards, when a big cat with blazing eyes came in through the wall and miawed out, '*Shone feol!*' (I want flesh). They were so frightened they gave him the quarter that was roasting. When he ate it he licked his chops and roared out again, '*Shone feol!*', and so on till he gobbled up all the sheep and three quarters of the cow. Hoping that he'd leave them a bit for themselves, they were boiling a piece of beef over the fire in the cows hide, stuck up on four stakes with some water in the hollow, but he bawled out more vicious than ever, when all the rest was down the red lane, '*Shone feol!*'

Well, they gave him the piece that was simmering, and while he was atn' it they got out and were making the road home as fast as they could. They were not a quarter of a mile away when the moon happened to show her face, the *bodach's* boy cried out, 'Master, master, the cat is sitting on the crupper behind you.' He turned round and was so wild with fright and anger, that he pushed at the tormentor with his pike over his left shoulder, and whether he was killed or not, down to the ground he came. *Ovoch!* In a moment you'd think all the cats from Blackstairs to Carrigbyrne were round them, and before they could look round, the boy and his horse were down, and the wild creatures tearing them limb from limb. The master set spurs to his horse while they were at their work, and never cried crack till he was inside his own bawn and the gate locked. He was more dead than alive when he got in, and couldn't tell what happened him for ever so long. At last he began to tell his wife an account of what happened, but when he came to the blow he made with the pike and the tumble of the cat, a kitten only half a year old that was sitting on a boss screamed out, 'Oh, you thief did you kill my uncle?' and without another word she flew at his throat, and tore out a piece the size of her own head. If he hadn't gone on a murdering business, his wife wouldn't be a widow from that day to the last one of her life.

15: THE LOVE PHILTRE (A Fact)

Nora, a healthy, bouncing young country damsel, but no way gifted with beauty, registered a vow that she would be the wife of young Mr Bligh, a 'half sir', that lived near. The young fellow always spoke civilly and good-naturedly to her, but after a year of two's acquaintance, Nora saw no immediate sign of her vow being accomplished. She held consultations with adepts in fairy and demon lore, and discovered that the liver of a cat thoroughly black, white paws excepted, was sovereign in the process of procuring a return of love. Aided by her sister and another woman, researches were made, the cat discovered, and slain, with accompaniments which we do not choose to particularise. The liver was then carefully taken out, broiled, and reduced to an impalpable powder.

In a day or two the gallant was passing by Nora's cottage, and seeing her at the bawn gate he 'put the speak' on her. She, nothing loth, kept up the conversation, and after some further talk, asked might she take the liberty of requesting him to come in and take a cup of tea. He did not think the better of her prudence for making the demand, but felt he couldn't refuse with incivility. So he was set comfortably at table, and Nora soon filled his cup from a black teapot, which, in addition to some indifferent tea, contained a pinch of philtre. The guest began the banquet with notions and intentions not very complimentary to his entertainer;

setting her up as the mistress of his heart and house. It is in the nature of this magic potion, that if the dose is not repeated at intervals, the effect becomes weaker, and at length ceases altogether. Nora, aware of this, renewed the administration at every visit, till his infatuation became such that he announced to his family and relations his immediate marriage with the cabin girl. Vain were the coaxings, threats, reasonings, etc.; and at last the eve of the wedding-day arrived. Paying a visit to his charmer that happy evening, they were enjoying the most interesting and delightful conversation, when the latch was raised, and a party of seven or eight young fellows, armed with good hazel rods, entered and began to lay thousands on his devoted back and shoulders. Nora flung herself between, and received a few slight blows; but before they ceased practising on the amorous youth, every bone in his body was sore, and he himself unable to use arms or legs. That was what they wanted. They trundled him into a car, and took him home, where he was tended and watched for a month. The drug not being administered all that time, he was amazed when he was able to quit his bed that he should ever have been guilty of such an absurdity. So to Nora's remorse for the unholy proceeding was now added chagrin at her want of success.

16: THE FAIRY CHILD

There was a sailor that lived up in Grange when he was at home, and one time, when he was away seven or eight months, his wife was brought to bed of a fine boy. She expected her husband back soon, and she wished to put off the christening of the child till he'd be on the spot. She and her husband were not natives of the country, and they were not as much afraid of leaving the child unchristened as our people would be.

Well, the child grew and throve, and the neighbours all bothered the woman to take him to Father M.'s to be baptised, and all they said was no use. 'Her husband would be soon home, and then they'd have a joyful christening.'

There happened to be no one sick up in that neighbourhood for some time, so the priest did not come to the place, nor hear of the birth, and none of the people about her could make up their minds to tell upon her, it is such an ugly thing to be informing; and then the child was so healthy, and the father might be on the spot any moment.

So the time crept on, and the lad was a year and a half old, and his mother up to that time never lost five nights' rest by him; when one evening that she came in from binding after the reapers, she heard wonderful whingeing and lamenting from the bed where he used to sleep. She ran over to him and asked him what ailed him. 'Oh, mammy, I'm sick, and I'm hungry, and I'm cold, don't pull down the blanket.' Well, the poor woman ran and got some boiled bread and milk as soon as she could, and she asked her other son, that was about seven years old, when he took sick. 'Oh, mother,' says he, 'he was as happy as a king, playing near the fire about two hours ago, and I was below in the room, when I heard a great rush like as if a whole number of fowls were flying down the chimney. I heard my brother giving a great cry, and then another sound like as if the fowls were flying out again; when I got into the kitchen there he was, so miserable-looking and his clothes, and his poor face so dirty. Take a look at him, and try do you know him at all.'

So when she went to feed him she got such a fright, for his poor face was like an old man's, and his body, and legs, and arms, all thin and hairy. But still he resembled the child she left in the morning, and 'mammy, mammy,' was never out of his mouth. She heard of people being fairy-struck, so she supposed it was that that happened to him, but she never suspected her own child to be gone, and a fairy child left in its place.

Well, it's he that kept the poor woman awake many a night after, and never let her have a quiet day, crying for bread and milk, and mashed potatoes, and stirabout; and it was still 'mammy, mammy, mammy,' and the glows and the moans were never out of his mouth. Well, he had like to eat the poor woman out of house and home, and the very flesh off her bones with watching and sorrow. Still nothing could persuade her that it wasn't her own child that was in it.

One neighbour and another neighbour told her

their minds plain enough. 'Now, ma'am, you see what it is to leave a child without being christened. If you done your duty, fairy, nor spirit, nor divel, would have no power over your child. That *ounkran* in the bed is no more your child nor I am, but a little imp that the *Daoine Sighe*—God between us and harm!—left you. By this and by that, if you don't whip him up and come along with us to Father M's, we'll go, hot foot, ourselves, and tell him all about it. Christened he must be before the day is older.'

So she went over and soothered him, and said, 'Come, alanna, let me dress you, and we'll go and be christened.' And such roaring and screeching as came out of this throat would frighten the Danes. 'I haven't the heart,' says she at last, 'and sure if we attempted to take him in that state we'd have the people of the three townlands following us to the priest's, and I'm afraid he'd take it very badly.'

The next day when she came in, in the evening, she found him quite clean and fresh-looking, and his hair nicely combed. 'Ah, Pat,' says she to her other son, 'was it you that done this?' Well, he said nothing till he and his mother were up at the fire, and the angashore of a child in his bed in the room. 'Mother,' says he then, in a whisper, 'the neighbours are right, and you are wrong. I was out a little bit, and when I was coming round by the wall at the back of the room, I heard some sweet voices as if they were singing inside; and so I went to the crack in the corner, and what was round the bed but a whole parcel of nicely-dressed little women, with green gowns, and they singing, and dressing the little fellow, and combing his hair, and he

49

laughing and crowing with them. I watched for a long time, and then I stole round to the door, but the moment I pulled the string of the latch I heard the music change to his whimpering and crying, and when I got into the room there was no sign of anything only himself. He was a little better looking, but as cantankerous as ever.' 'Ah,' says the mother, 'you are only joining the ill-natured neighbours. You're not telling a word of truth.'

Next day Pat had a new story. 'Mother,' says he, 'I was sitting here while you were out, and I began to wonder why he was so quiet, so I went into the room to see if he was asleep. There he was, sitting up with his old face on him, and he frightened the life out of me, he spoke so plain. "Paudh," says he, "go and light your mother's pipe, and let me have a shough; I'm tired o' my life lying here." "Ah, you thief," says I, "wait till you hear what she'll say to you when I tell her this." "Tell away, you pickthanks," says he, "she won't believe a word you say."' 'And neither do I believe one word from you,' said the mother.

At last a letter came from the father, saying he'd be home after the letter as soon as coaches and ships could carry him. 'Now,' says the poor woman, 'we'll have the christening anyway.' So the next day she went to New Ross to buy sugar and tay, and beef and pork, to give a grand let-out to welcome her husband, but bedad the long-headed neighbours took the opportunity to gain their ends of the fairy imp. They gathered round the house, and one stout woman came up to the bed, promiskis-like, and wrapped him up in the quilt before he had time to defend himself, and away down the lane to the Boro she went, and the whole townland at her heels. He thought to get away, but she held him pinned as if he was in a vice, and he kept roaring, and the crowd kept laughing, and they never crack-cried till they were at the stepping-stones going to Ballybawn from Grange.

Well, when he felt himself near the water he roared like a score of bulls, and kicked like the divel, but my brave woman wasn't to be daunted. She got on the first stepping-stone, and water, as black as night from the turf-mould running under her. He felt as heavy as lead, but she held on to the second. Well, she thought she'd go down there with the roaring, and the weight, and the dismal colour of the river, but she got to the middlestone, and there down through the quilt he fell as a heavy stone would through a muslin handkerchief. Off he went, whirling round and round, and letting the frightfulest laughs out of him, and showing his teeth and cracking his fingers at the people on the banks. 'Oh, yous think yous are very clever, now,' says he. 'You may tell that fool of a woman from me that all I'm sorry for is that I didn't choke her, or do worse for her, before her husband comes home; bad luck to yous all!'

Well, they all came back joyful enough, though they were a little frightened. But weren't they rejoiced to meet the poor woman running to them with her fine healthy child in her arms, that she found in a delightful sleep when she got back from the town. You may be sure the next day didn't pass over him till he was baptised, and the next day his father got safe home. Well, I needn't say how happy they were; but bedad the woman was a little ashamed of herself next Sunday at Rathnure Chapel while Father James was preaching about the wickedness of neglecting to get young babies baptised as soon as possible after they're born.

17: THE CHANGELING AND HIS BAGPIPES

A certain youth whom we shall here distinguish by the name of Rickard the Rake, amply earned his title by the time he lost in fair-tents, in dance-houses, in following hunts, and other unprofitable occupations, leaving his brothers and his aged father to attend to the concerns of the farm, or neglect them as they pleased. It is indispensable to the solemnities of a night dance in the country, to take the barn door off its hinges, and lay in on the floor to test the skill of the best dancers in the room in a single performance. In this was Rickard eminent, and many an evening did he hold the eyes of the assembly intent on his flourishes, lofty springs and kicks, and the other fashionable variations taught by the departed race of dancing-masters.

One evening while earning the applause of the admiring crowd, he uttered a cry of pain, and fell on his side on the hard door. A wonderful scene of confusion ensued—the groans of the dancer, the pitying exclamations of the crowd, and their endeavours to stifle the sufferer in their eagerness to comfort him. We must suppose him carried home and confined to his bed for weeks, the complaint being a stiffness in one of his hip joints, occasioned by a fairy-dart. Fairy-doctors, male and female, tried their herbs and charms on him in vain, and more than one on leaving the house said to one of his family, 'God send it's not one of the *sheeoges* yous are nursing, instead of poor wild Rickard!'

And indeed there seemed to be some reason in the observation. The jovial, reckless, good-humoured buck was now a meagre, disagreeable, exacting creature, with pinched features, and harsh voice, and craving appetite, and for several weeks he continued to plague and distress his unfortunate family. By the advice of a fairy-man a pair of bagpipes was accidentally left near his bed, and ears were soon on the stretch to catch the dulcet notes of the instrument from the room. It was well known that he was not at all skilled in the musical art; so if a well-played tune were heard from under his fingers, the course to be adopted by this family was clear.

But the invalid was as crafty as they were cunning; groans of pain and complaints of neglect formed the only body of sound that issued from the sick chamber. At last, during a hot harvest afternoon when everyone should be in the field, and a dead silence reigned through the house, and yard, and outoffices, someone that was watching from an unsuspected press saw an anxious, foxy face peep out from the gently opened door of the room, and draw itself back after a careful survey of the great parlour into which it opened, and which had the large kitchen on the other side. Soon after, the introductory squeal of the instrument was heard, but of a sweeter quality than the same pipes ever uttered before or after that day. Then followed a strain of such wild and sweet melody as held in silent rapture about a dozen of the people of the house who had been apprised of the experiment, and who, till the first enchanting sound breathed

54

through the house, had kept themselves quiet in the room above the kitchen, consequently the farthest from the changeling's station.

While they stood or sat entranced as air succeeded air, and the last still the sweetest, they began to distinguish whispers, and the nearly inaudible rustle of soft and gauzy dresses seemingly brushing against each other, and such subdued sounds as a cat's feet might cause, swiftly pacing along a floor. They were unable to stir, or even move their lips, so powerful was the charm of the fairy's music on their wills and their senses, till at last the fairy-man spoke—the only person who had the will or the capacity to hold conference with him being the fairy-woman from the next townland.

He — Come, come; this must be put a stop to.

The words were not all uttered when a low whistling noise was heard from the next room, and the moment after there was a profound stillness.

She — Yes, indeed; and what would you advise us to do first with the anointed *sheeoge*?

He — We'll begin easy. We'll take him neck and crop and hold his head under the water in the turn-hold till we'll drive the divel out of him.

She — That 'ud be a great deal too easy a punishment for the thief. We'll heat the shovel red-hot, put it under his currabingo, and land him out in the dung-lough.

He —Ah, now, can't you try easier punishments on him? I'll put the tongs in the fire till the claws are as hot as the divel, and won't I hould his nasty crass nose between them till he'll know the difference between fiery faces and a latchycock.

She —No, no! Say nothing, and I'll go and bring

my liquor, drawn from the leaves of the *lussmore*, and if he was a sheeoge forty times, it will put the inside of him into such a state that he'd give the world if he could die. Some parts of him will be as if he had red-hot saws rasping him asunder, and others as if needles of ice were crossing and crossing each other in his bowels; and when he's dead, we'll give him no better grave nor the bog-hole, or the outside of the churchyard.

He —Very well, let's begin. I'll bring my red-hot tongs from the kitchen fire, and you your little bottle of lussmore water. Don't any of yez go in, neighbours, till we have them ingredients ready.

There was a pause in the outer room while the fairy-man passed into the kitchen and back. Then there was a rush at the door, and a bursting into the room. But there was no sign of the changeling on the bed, nor under the bed, nor in any part of the room. At last one of the women shouted out in terror, for the face of the fiend was seen at the window, looking in, with such scorn and hate on the fearful features as struck terror into the boldest. However, the fairy-man dashed at him with his burning tongs in hand; but just as it was on the point of gripping his nose, a something between a laugh and a scream, that made the blood in their veins run cold, came from him. Face and all vanished, and that was the last that was seen of him. Next morning, Rickard, now a reformed rake, was found in his own bed. Great was the joy at his recovery, and great it continued, for he laid aside his tobacco pipe, and pint and quart measures. He forsook the tent and the sheebeen house, and took kindly to his reaping-hook, his spade, his plough,

and his prayer book, and blessed the night he was
fairy-struck on the dance floor.

18: THE TOBINSTOWN SHEEOGE

In the pleasant valley of the Duffrey, sheltered from the north-west winds by the huge pile of Mount Leinster, lie two villages separated by a turf bog. The western cluster is called Kennystown, and the eastern, Tobinstown. The extensive Rath of Cromogue commands the bog on the north, and the over-abounding moisture in the holes and drains finds its way to the noisy Glasha on the south. The elder inhabitants of these villages spoke the Irish tongue at the close of the last century and the beginning of this. About the year 1809, the inhabitants of the whole valley spent a Sunday afternoon on the dry tussocks of the bog, sounding the dark pools with long poles and fishing spears, to stir up a descendant of the serpent that had laid the country waste in the days of Brian Boru. Some intelligent person had seen it lying on the surface of Lough na Piastha about half a mile off, a day or two before, and a still more intelligent person had seen it tearing across the intermediate fields on Saturday night, with sparks of fire flashing from its tail. If the young piast was at the bottom of a bog-hole he remained there quietly enough. The enthusiastic crowd was obliged to separate at nightfall, no incident having rewarded their expectations beyond the fall of a little boy into a turfpool, his rescue and consequent punishment by a loving but irritable parent. This, however, is no better than a digression.

Katty Clarke of Tobinstown was once happy in the possession of a fine boy, the delight of her eyes and heart, till one unlucky day, when she happened to sleep too long in the morning, and, consequently, had not time to say her prayers. Mr Clarke, coming in from the fields, was annoyed at not finding the stirabout ready, and opened his mind on the subject. Katty was vexed with him and herself, and cursed a little, as was customary sixty years since among men and women in remote districts of our country. All these annoyances prevented her from remembering the holy water, and from sprinkling some drops on her little son, and making the sign of the cross on his innocent forehead. When the men and boys left the house for their outdoor work after breakfast, Katty took a pailful of soiled linen to the spot where the stream formed a little pool, and where the villagers had fixed a board and flat 'beetling' stone. While she was employed in cleaning the clothes, she let her child sit or roll about on the grassy slope behind her.

All at once she heard a scream from the boy, and when she turned, and ran to him, she found him in convulsions. She ran home with him, administered salt and water, and other specifics popular in the country. The fit passed away, but she was grieved to perceive that the weazened, pained expression still remained on his face, and that his whimpering and whining did not abate—in fact, to use a well-worn Irish expression, 'the cry was never out of his mouth.' He ate as much as would suffice a full-grown man, and was always ready for food both at regular mealtimes and between them. After a week of this state of things, the neighbours came to the conclusion that it was a sheeoge that Katty was slaving her life out for. Katty's family came next into the same persuasion, and lastly, but with some doubts, Katty herself.

At a family and neighbourly council, held round the fire, after the children had been sent to bed, they proceeded to get rid of the little wretch, and this was the order of the ceremonial:

A neighbour took the shovel, rubbed it clean, laid it on the floor, and his wife, seizing on the supposed fairy, placed it sitting on the broad iron blade. She held it there stoutly, notwithstanding its howls, while her husband, raising it gently, proceeded to the bawn, accompanied by the assembly, and, despite all opposition on its part, placed it on a wisp of straw which crowned the manure heap. The luxury of the seat did not succeed in arresting his outcries, but his audience not taking much notice, joined hands, and in their own parlance serenaded the crowned heap three times, while the fairy-man, who had been summoned from Bawnard (high court), recited an incantation in Irish, of which we give a literal version:

Come at our call, O Sighe mother!
Come and remove your offspring.
Food and drink he has received,
And kindness from the *Ben-a-teagh*.
Here he no longer shall stay,
But depart to the *Daoine Matha*.
Restore the lost child, O *Bean-Sighe*!
And food shall be left for thy people
When the cloth is spread on the harvest field,
On the short grass newly mown.
Food shall be left on the dresser-shelf,

And the hearthstone shall be clean,
When the *Clann Sighe* come in crowds,
And sweep in rings round the floor,
And hold their feast at the fire.
Restore the mortal child, O *Bean-Sighe*!
And receive thine own at our hands.

They soon felt the air around them sweep this way
and that, as if it was stirred by the motion of wings,
but they remained quiet and silent for about ten
minutes. Opening the door, they then looked out,
and saw the bundle of straw on the heap, but
neither child nor fairy. 'Go into your bedroom,
Katty,' said the fairy-man, 'and see if there's anything left on the bed.' She did so, and they soon
heard a cry of joy, and Katty was among them in a
moment, kissing and hugging her own healthy-look-
ing child, who was waking and rubbing his eyes, and
wondering at the lights and all the eager faces.

Whatever hurry Katty might be in of a morning
after that, she never left her bedside till she had
finished, as devoutly as she could, her five Paters
and five Aves, and her Apostles' Creed and her
Confiteor. And she never cursed or swore except
when she was surprised by a sudden fit of passion.

19: THE BELATED PRIEST

A very lonesome road connects the village of Ballindaggin, in the Duffrey, with the townland of Mangan, on the Bantry side of the brawling Urrin, and outside these intermediate stations it leads to Kaim and Castleboro, on one side and the high road from Bunclody to Ross on the other. From the river to Ballindaggin, you hardly meet a house, and fallow fields extend on each side.

Father Stafford was asked, rather late in the day, to make a sick call at a cabin that stood among these fields, at a considerable distance from this road—a cabin from which no lane led either to by-road or public road. He was delayed longer than he expected, and when he was leaving the cabin it was nearly dark. This did not disturb him much. There was a path that led to the road, and he knew he had only to keep a north-easterly direction to come out on it, not far from the village already named. So he went on fearlessly for some time, but complete obscurity soon surrounded him, and he would have been sorely perplexed, had it not been that the path lay for the most part beside the fences.

At last, instead of passing in a line near the fence, it struck across the field; and, open his eyes wide as he might, he could hardly distinguish it from the dry, russet-coloured grass at each side. Well, he kept his eyes steadily fixed in the due direction, and advanced till he was about the middle of the field, which happened to be a large one. There some case of conscience, or other anxious subject, crossed his mind, and he stopped and fidgeted about, walking restlessly this way and that for a few steps, totally forgetting his present circumstances. Coming at last to some solution of his difficulty, full recollection returned, and he was sensible of being thoroughly ignorant of the direction in which his proper route lay. If he could but get a glimpse of Mount Leinster, it would be all well; but, beyond a few perches, all was in the deepest darkness on every side. He then set off in a straight line, which he knew would bring him to some fence, and perhaps he might find stile or gap for his guidance. He went twice round the field, but, in the confusion of his faculties, he could find no trace of path or pass. He at last resolved to cross the fence, and go straight on, but the dykes were, for the most part, encumbered with briers, and furze-bushes crowned the tops of the steep clay mounds.

While he stood perplexed, he heard the rustle of wings or bodies passing swiftly through the air, and a musical voice was heard, 'You will suffer much if you do not find your way. Give us a favourable answer to a question, and you shall be on the road in a few minutes.' The good priest was somewhat awed at the rustle and the voice, but he answered without delay, 'Who are you, and what's your question?' The same voice replied, 'We are the Clann Sighe, and wish you to declare that at the last day our lot may not be with Satan. Say that the Saviour died for us as well as for you.' 'I will give you a favourable answer, if you can make me a hopeful one. Do you adore and love the Son of God?' He received no answer but weak and shrill cries, and the rushing of wings, and at once it seemed as if he had shaken off some oppression. The dark clouds had separated, a weak light was shed round where he stood, and he distinguished the path, and an opening in the bushes on the fence. He crossed into the next field, and, following the path, he was soon on the road. In fifteen minutes he was seated at his comfortable fire, and his little round table, covered with books, was at his side.

20: THE PALACE IN THE RATH

Every one from Bunclody to Enniscorthy knows the rath between Tombrick and Munfin. Well, there was a poor, honest, quiet little creature, that lived just at the pass of Glanamoin, between the hill of Coolgarrow and Kilachdiarmid. His back was broken when he was a child, and he earned his bread by making cradles, and bosses, and chairs, and beehives, out of straw and briars. No one in the barony of Bantry or Scarawalsh could equal him at these. Well, he was a sober little fellow enough, but the best of us may be overtaken. He was coming from the fair of Enniscorthy one fine summer evening, up along the beautiful shady road of Munfin, and when he came near the stream that bounds Tombrick, he turned into the fields to make his road short. He was singing merrily enough, but by degrees he got a little stupefied, and when he was passing the dry, grassy ditch that surrounds the rath, he felt an inclination to sit and rest himself.

It is hard to sit awhile, and have your eyes a little glassy, and the things seeming to turn round you, without falling off asleep; and asleep my poor little man of straw was in a few minutes. Things like droves of cattle, or soldiers marching, or big flakes of foam on a flooded river, were pushing on through his brain, and he thought the drums were playing a march, when up he woke, and there in the face of the steep bank that was overgrown with bushes and blackthorn, a passage was open between nice pillars, and inside a great vaulted room, with arches crossing each other, a hundred lamps hanging from the vault, and thousands of nice little gentlemen and ladies, with green coats and gowns, and red sugar-loaf caps, curled at the tops like old Irish birredhs, dancing and singing, and nice little pipers and fiddlers, perched up in a little gallery by themselves, and playing music to help out the singing.

He was a little cowed at first, but as he found no one taking notice of him, he stole in, and sat in a corner, and thought he'd never be tired looking at the fine little people figuring, and cutting capers, and singing. But at last he began to find the singing and music a little tedious. It was nothing but two short bars and four words, and this was the style:

Yae Luan, yae Morth
Yae Luan, yae Morth.

The longer he looked on, the bolder he grew, and at last he shouted at the end of the verse:

Agus Dha Haed-yeen.

Oh, such cries of delight as rose up among the merry little gentry! They began the improved song, and shouted till the vault rang:

Yae Luan, yae Morth—
Yae Luan, yae Morth—
Yae Luan, yae Morth.
Agus Dha Haed-yeen.

After a few minutes, they all left off the dance, and gathered round the boss maker, and thanked him for improving their tune. 'Now,' said the chief, 'if you wish for anything, only say the word, and, if it is in our power, it must be done.' 'I thank you, ladies and gentlemen,' says he, 'and if you would only remove this hump from my back, I'd be the happiest man in the Duffrey.' 'Oh, easy done, easy done!' said they. 'Go on again with the dance, and you come along with us.' So on they went with:

Monday, Tuesday—
Monday, Tuesday—
Monday, Tuesday,
    And Wednesday too.

One fairy taking their new friend by the heel, shot him in a curve to the very roof, and down he came the other side of the hall. Another gave him a shove, and up he flew back again. He felt as if he had wings; and one time when his back touched the roof, he found a sudden delightful change in himself; and just as he touched the ground, he lost all memory of everything around him. Next morning he was awakened by the sun shining on his face from over Slieve Buie, and he had a delightful feel down along his body instead of the disagreeable *cruith* he was accustomed to. He felt as if he could go from that to the other side of the stream at one step, and he burned little daylight till he reached Glanamoin. He had some trouble to persuade the neighbours of the truth of what had happened; but the wonder held only nine days; and he had like to lose his health along with his hump, for if he only made his appearance in Ballycarney, Castle-Dockrell, Ballindaggin, Kilmeashil, or Bunclody, ten people would be inviting him to a share of a tumbler of punch, or a quart of mulled beer.

The news of the wonderful cure was talked of high and low, and even went as far as Ballynocrish, in Bantry, where another poor *angashore* of a humpback lived. But he was very unlike the Duffrey man in his disposition: he was as cross as a brier, and almost begrudged his right hand to help his left. His poor old aunt and a neighbour of hers set out one day, along with him, along the Bunclody road, passing by Killanne and the old place of the Colcloughs at Duffrey Hall, till they reached Templeshambo. Then they kept along the hilly by-road till they reached the little man's house near the pass.

So they up and told their business, and he gave them a kind welcome, and explained all the ins and outs of his adventure; and the end was, the four went together in the heel of the evening to the rath, and left the little lord in his glory in the dry, brown grass of the round dyke, where the other met his good fortune. The little ounkran never once thanked them for all the trouble they were taking for him. He only whimpered about being left in that lonesome place, and bade them to be sure to be with him at the flight of night, because he did not know what way to take from it.

At last, the poor cross creature fell asleep; and after dreaming about falling down from rocks, and being held over the sea by his hump, and then that a lion had him by the same hump, and was running away with him, and then that it was put up for a target for soldiers to shoot at, the first volley they gave awoke him, and what was it but the music of the fairies in full career. The melody was the same as it was left them by the hive-maker, and the tune and dancing was twice as good as it was at first. This is the way it went:

Yae Luan, yae Morth—
Yae Luan, yae Morth—
Yae Luan, yae Morth,
  Agus Dha Haed-yeen.

But the new visitor had neither taste nor discretion; so when they came about the third time to the last line, he croaked out:

Agus Dha Yaerd-yeen,
Agus Dha Haen-ya.

It was the same as a cross fiddler that finds nobody going to give him anything, and makes a harsh back-screak of his bow along one of the strings. A thousand voices cried out, 'Who stops our dance? Who stops our dance?' and all gathered round the poor fellow. He could do nothing but stare at them with his poor, cross, frightened face; and they screamed and laughed till he thought it was all over with him.

But is was not over with him.

'Bring down that hump,' says the king; and before you could kiss your hand it was clapped on, as fast as the knocker of Newgate, over the other hump. The music was over now, the lights went out, and the poor creature lay till morning in a nightmare; and there the two women found him, at daybreak, more dead than alive. It was a dismal return they had to Ballynocrish; and the moral of my story is, that you should never drive till you first try the virtue of leading.

21: THE FAIRY NURSE

There was once a little farmer and his wife living
near Coolgarrow. They had three children and my
story happened while the youngest was on the
breast. The wife was a good wife enough, but her
mind was all on her family and her farm, and she
hardly ever went to her knees without falling asleep,
and she thought the time spent in the chapel was
twice as long as it need be. So, begonies, she let her
man and her two children go before her one day to
Mass, while she called to consult a fairy-man about
a disorder one of her cows had. She was late at the
chapel, and was sorry all the day after, for her husband was in grief about it, and she was very fond
of him.

Late that night he was wakened up by the cries
of his children calling out, 'Mother, Mother!' When
he sat up and rubbed his eyes, there was no wife by
his side, and when he asked the little ones what
was become of their mother, they said they saw
the room full of nice little men and women, dressed in white, and red, and green, and their mother
in the middle of them, going out by the door as if
she was walking in her sleep. Out he ran, and
searched everywhere round the house, but neither
tale nor tidings did he get of her for many a day.

Well, the poor man was miserable enough, for he
was as fond of his woman as she was of him. It
used to bring the salt tears down his cheeks to see
his poor children neglected and dirty, as they often

were, and they'd be bad enough only for a kind neighbour that used to look in whenever she could spare time. The infant was out with a wet nurse.

About six weeks after—just as he was going out to his work one morning—a neighbour, that used to mind women at their lying-in, came up to him, and kept step by step with him to the field, and this is what she told him.

'Just as I was falling asleep last night, I hears a horse's tramp in the bawn, and a knock at the door, and there, when I came out, was a fine-looking dark man, mounted on a black horse, and he told me to get ready in all haste, for a lady was in great want of me. As soon as I put on my cloak and things, he took me by the hand, and I was sitting behind him before I felt myself stirring. "Where are we going, sir?" says I. "You'll soon know," says he, and he drew his fingers across my eyes, and not a *stim* remained in them. I kept a tight grip of him, and the dickens a knew I knew whether he was going backwards or forwards, or how long we were about it, till my hand was taken again, and I felt the ground under me. The fingers went the other way across my eyes, and there we were before a castle door, and in we went through a big hall and great rooms all painted in fine green colours, with red and gold bands and ornaments, and the finest carpets and chairs and tables and window curtains, and fine ladies and gentlemen walking about. At last we came to a bedroom, with a beautiful lady in bed, and there he left me with her, and, bedad, it was not long till a fine bouncing boy came into the world. The lady clapped her hands, and in came *Fir Dhorocha*, and kissed her and his son, and

71

praised me, and gave me a bottle of green ointment to rub the child all over.

Well, the child I rubbed, sure enough, but my right eye began to smart me, and I put up my finger and gave it a rub, and purshuin to me if ever I was so frightened. The beautiful room was a big rough cave, with water oozing over the edges of the stones, and through the clay; and the lady, and the lord, and the child, weazened, poverty-bitten crathurs—nothing but skin and bone, and rich dresses were old rags. I didn't let on that I found any difference, and after a bit says *Fir Dhorocha*, "Go before me to the hall-door, and I will be with you in a few moments, and see you safe home." Well, just as I turned into the outside cave, who should I see watching near the door but poor Molly. She looked round all frightened, and she says to me in a whisper—"I'm brought here to give suck to the child of the king and queen of the fairies; but there is one chance of saving me. All the court will pass the cross of Templeshambo, next Friday night, on a visit to the fairies of Old Ross. If John can catch me by the hand or cloak when I ride by, and has courage not to let go his grip, I'll be safe. Here's the king. Don't open your mouth to answer. I saw what happened with the ointment."

'*Fir Dhorocha* didn't once cast his eye towards Molly, and he seemed to have no suspicion of me. When we came out I looked about me, and where do you think we were but in the dyke of the Rath of Cromogue. I was on the horse again, which was nothing but a big *boolian bui*, and I was in dread every minute I'd fall off; but nothing happened till I found myself in my own bawn. The king slipped ive guineas into my hands as soon as I was on the ground, and thanked me, and bade me good night. I hope I'll never see his face again. I got into bed, and couldn't sleep for a long time; and when I examined my five guineas this morning, that I left in the table-drawer the last thing, I found five withered leaves of oak—bad scran to the giver!'

Well, you may all think the fright, and the joy, and the grief the poor man was in when the woman finished her story. They talked, and they talked, but we needn't mind what they said till Friday night came, when both were standing where the mountain road crosses the one going to Ross.

There they stood looking towards the bridge of Thuar, and I won't keep you waiting, as they were in the dead of night, with a little moonlight shining from over Kilachdiarmid. At last she gave a start and 'By this and by that,' says she, 'here they come, bridles jingling, and feathers tossing,' He looked, but could see nothing; and she stood trembling, and her eyes wide open, looking down the way to the ford of Ballinacoola. 'I see your wife,' says she, 'riding on the outside just so as to rub against us. We'll walk on promiskis-like, as if we suspected nothing, and when we are passing I'll give you a shove. If you don't do your duty then dickens cure you!'

Well, they walked on easy, and the poor hearts beating in both their breasts; and though he could see nothing, he heard a faint jingle, and tramping, and rustling, and at last he got the push that she promised. He spread out his arms, and there was his wife's waist within them, and he could see her plain, but such a hullabuloo rose as if there was an earthquake; and he found himself surrounded by horrible looking things, roaring at him, and striving to pull his wife away. But he made the sign of the cross, and bid them begone in God's name, and held his wife as if it was iron his arms were made of. Bedad, in one moment everything was as silent as the grave, and the poor woman lying in a faint in the arms of her husband and her good neighbour. Well, all in good time she was minding her family and her business again, and I'll go bail, after the fright she got, she spent more time on her knees, and avoided the fairy-men all the days of the week, and particularly Sunday.

It is hard to have anything to do with the good people without getting a mark from them. My brave midwife didn't escape no more nor another. She was one Thurdsay at the market of Enniscorthy, when what did she see walking among the tubs of butter but *Fir Dhorocha*, very hungry-looking, and taking a scoop out of one tub and out of another. 'Oh, sir,' says she, very foolish, 'I hope your lady is well, and the young heir.' 'Pretty well, thank you,' says he, rather frightened like. 'How do I look in this new suit?' says he, getting to one side of her. 'I can't see you plain at all, sir,' says she. 'Well, now,' says he, getting round her back to the other side. 'Musha, indeed, sir, your coat looks no better nor a withered dock-leaf.' 'Maybe, then,' says he, 'it will be different now,' and he struck the eye next him with a switch.

Begonies, she never saw a *stim* after with that one till the day of her death.

22: THE RECOVERED BRIDE

There was a marriage in the townland of Curra-
graigue. After the usual festivities, and when the
guests were left to themselves, and were drinking
to the prosperity of the bride and bridegroom,
they were startled by the appearance of the man
himself rushing into the room with anguish in his
looks. 'Oh,' cried he, 'Margaret is carried away by
the fairies, I'm sure. The girls were not left the
room for half a minute when I went in, and there
is no more sign of her there than if she never was
born.' Great consternation prevailed, great search
was made, but no Margaret was to be found. After
a night and day spent in misery, the poor bridegroom laid down to take some rest. In a while he
seemed to himself to wake from a troubled dream,
and look out into the room. The moon was shining
in through the window, and in the middle of the
slanting rays stood Margaret in her white bridal
clothes. He thought to speak and leap out of bed,
but his tongue was without utterance, and his
limbs unable to move. 'Do not be disturbed, dear
husband,' said the appearance, 'I am now in the
power of the fairies, but if you only have courage
and prudence we may be soon happy with each
other again. Next Friday will be May Eve, and the
whole court will ride out of the old fort at midnight.
I must be there along with the rest. Sprinkle a
circle with holy water, and have a black-hafted
knife with you. If you have courage to pull me off

the horse, and draw me into the ring, all they can do will be useless. You must have some food for me every night on the dresser, for if I taste one mouthful with them, I will be lost to you for ever. The fairies got power over me because I was only thinking of you, and did not prepare myself as I ought for the sacrament. I made a bad confession, and now I am suffering for it. Don't forget what I have said.' 'Oh, no, my darling,' cried he, recovering his speech, but by the time he had slipped out of bed, there was no living soul in the room but himself.

Till Friday night the poor young husband spent a desolate time. The food was left on the dresser over night, and it rejoiced all hearts to find it vanished by morning. A little before midnight he was at the entrance of the old rath. He formed the circle, took his station within it, and kept the black-hafted knife ready for service. At times he was nervously afraid of losing his dear wife, and at others burning with impatience for the struggle. At last the old fort with its dark high bushy fences cutting against the sky, was in a moment replaced by a palace and its court. A thousand lights flashed from the windows and lofty hall entrance, numerous torches were brandished by attendants stationed round the courtyard, and a numerous cavalcade of richly-attired ladies and gentlemen was moving in the direction of the gate where he found himself standing. As they rode by him laughing and jesting, he could not tell whether they were aware of his presence or not. He looked intent at each countenance as it approached, but it was some time before he caught sight of the dear face and figure borne along on a milk-white steed. She recognised him well enough, and her features now broke into a smile—now expressed deep anxiety. She was unable for the throng to guide the animal close to the ring of power, so he suddenly rushed out of his bounds, seized her in his arms, and lifted her off. Cries of rage and fury arose on every side; they were hemmed in, and weapons were directed at his head and breast to terrify him. He seem to be inspired with superhuman courage and force, and wielding the powerful knife he soon cleared a space around him, all seeming dismayed by the sight of the weapon. He lost no time, but drew his wife within the ring, within which none of the myriads round dared to enter. Shouts of derision and defiance continued to fill the air for some time, but the expedition could not be delayed. As the end of the procession filed past the gate and the circle within which the mortal pair held each other determinedly clasped, darkness and silence fell on the old rath and the fields round it, and the rescued bride and her lover breathed freely. We will not detain the sensitive reader on the happy walk home, on the joy that hailed their arrival, and on all the eager gossip that occupied the townland and the five that surround it for a month after the happy rescue.

23: FACTION-FIGHT AMONG THE FAIRIES

'I was sitting on the brow of that hill, the other day, and it was so calm you could hear the buzzing of a fly's wing. I was half-asleep with the heat and with having nothing to do, when I was aroused by a noise coming down from the mountain along the stream. The road crosses it just above the glen, and at the bridge the sound divided itself, and I heard the beat of wings on one side of the stream and on the other, but I could see nothing. I then seemed to hear the blowing of weak-voiced bugles, and faint shouts, and the sound of blows, as if two winged armies were fighting in the air; and even the firing of shots; but it was as if I was hearing all through a skreen or in a dream. It seemed to me even as if light bodies fell in the water. At last there was a greater shouting and work on one side, and hurraing, and then all the noise and rout rose in the air, and everything fell into quiet again. Fairies don't cross streams, you say! How then could the Leinster fairies cross over the Suir and Barrow to have a hurling match with the Munster fairies, or the fairies of Ireland have a battle with the Scotch fairies?'

24: JEMMY DOYLE IN THE FAIRY PALACE

My father was once coming down Scollagh Gap on a dark night, and all at once he saw, right before him, the lights coming from ever so many windows of a castle, and heard the shouts and laughing of people within. The door was wide open, and in he walked; and there on the spot where he had often drunk a tumbler of bad beer, he found himself in a big hall, and saw the king and queen of the fairies sitting at the head of a long table, and hundreds of people, all grandly dressed, eating and drinking. The clothes they had on them were of an old fashion, and there were harpers and pipers by themselves up in a gallery, and playing the most delightful old Irish airs. There was nothing to be seen but rich silk dresses, and pearls, and diamonds on the gentlemen and ladies and rich hangings on the walls, and lamps blazing.

The queen, as soon as she saw my father cried out, 'Welcome, Mr Doyle, make room there for Mr Doyle, and let him have the best at the table. Hand Mr Doyle a tumbler of punch, that will be strong and sweet. Sit down, Mr Doyle, and make yourself welcome.' So he sat down, and took the tumbler, and just as he was going to taste it, his eye fell on the man next him, and he was an old neighbour that was dead twenty years. Says the old neighbour, 'For your life, don't touch bit nor sup.' The smell was very nice, but he was frightened by what the dead neighbour said, and he began to notice how ghastly some of the fine people looked when they thought he was not minding them.

So his health was drunk, and he was pressed by the queen to fall to, but he had the sense to take the neighbour's advice, and only spilled the drink down between his coat and waistcoat.

At last the queen called for a song, and one of the guests sang a very indecent one in Irish. He often repeated a verse of it for us, but we didn't know the sense. At last he got sleepy, and recollected nothing more only the rubbing of his legs against the bushes in the *knoc* above our place in Cromogue; and we found him asleep next morning in the haggard, with a scent of punch from his mouth. He told us that we would get his knee-buckles on the path at the upper end of the *knoc*, and there, sure enough, they were found. Heaven be his bed!

25: THE SILKIE WIFE

Those in Shetland and Orkney Islands who know no better, are persuaded that the seals, or silkies, as they call them, can doss their coverings at times, and disport themselves as men and women. A fisher once turning a ridge of rock, discovered a beautiful bit of green turf ajoining the shingle sheltered by rocks on the land-ward side, and over this turf and shingle two beautiful women chasing each other, Just at the man's feet lay two sealskins, one of which he took up to examine it. The women, catching sight of him, screamed out, and ran to get possession of the skins. One seized the article on the ground, donned it in a thrice, and plunged into the sea; the other wrung her hands, cried, and begged the fisher to restore her property; but he wanted a wife, and would not throw away the chance. He wooed her so earnestly and lovingly, that she put on some woman's clothing which he brought her from his cottage, followed him home, and became his wife. Some years later, when their home was enlivened by the presence of two children, the husband awaking one night, heard voices in conversation from the kitchen. Stealing softly to the room door, he heard his wife talking in a low tone with some-one outside the window. The interview was just at an end, and he had only time to ensconce himself in bed, when his wife was stealing across the room. He was greatly disturbed, but determined to do or say nothing till he should acquire further knowledge. Next evening, as he was returning home by the strand, he spied a male and female *phoca* sprawling on a rock a few yards out at sea. The rougher animal, raising himself on his tail and fins, thus addressed the astonished man in the dialect spoken in these islands; 'You deprived me of her whom I was to make my companion; and it was only yesternight that I discovered her outer garment, the loss of which obliged her to be your wife. I bear no malice, as you were kind to her in your own fashion. Besides, my heart is too full of joy to hold any malice. Look on your wife for the last time.' The other seal glanced to him with all the shyness and sorrow she could force into her now uncouth features; but when the bereaved husband rushed toward the rock to secure his lost treasure, she and her companion were in the water on the other side of it in a moment, and the poor fisherman was obliged to return sadly to his motherless children and desolate home.

26: THE KILDARE POOKA

Mr H—— R——, when he was alive, used to live a good deal in Dublin, and he was once a great while out of the country on account of the 'Ninety-eight' business. But the servants kept on in the big house were all the same as if the family was at home. Well, they used to be frightened out of their lives after going to their beds, with the banging of the kitchen door and the clattering of the fire-irons, and the pots, and plates, and dishes. One evening they sat up ever so long, keeping one another in heart with telling stories about ghosts and fetches and that when—what would you have of it?—the little scullery boy that used to be sleeping over the horses, and couldn't get room at the fire, crept into the hot hearth, and when he got tired listening to the stories sorra fear him but he fell dead asleep.

Well and good, after they were all gone, and the fire raked up, he was woke with the noise of the kitchen door opening, and the trampling of an ass on the kitchen floor. He peeped out, and what should he see but a big grey ass, sure enough, sitting on his currabingo, and yawning before the fire. After a little, he looked about him, and began scratching his ears as if he was quite tired, and says he, 'I may as well begin first as last.' The poor boy's teeth began to chatter in his head, for says he, 'Now he's goin' to ate me,' but the fellow with the long ears and tail on him, had something else to do. He stirred up the fire, and then he brought in a pail

83

of water from the pump and filled a big pot, that he put on the fire before he went out. He then put in his hand—foot, I mean—into the hot hearth, and pulled out the little boy. He let a roar out of him with the fright, but the pooka only looked at him, and thrust out his lower lip to show how little he valued him, and then he pitched him into his pew again.

Well, he then lay down before the fire till he heard the boil coming on the water, and maybe there wasn't a plate, or a dish, or a spoon on the dresser, that he didn't fetch and put into the pot, and wash and dry the whole bilin' of 'em as well as e'er a kitchenmaid from that to Dublin town. He then put all of them up in their places on their shelves, and, if he didn't give a good sweepin' to the kitchen after all, leave it till again. Then he comes and sits foment the boy, let down one of his ears and cocked up the other, and gave a grin. The poor fellow strove to roar out, but not a *dheeg* 'ud come out of his throat. The last thing the pooka done was to rake up the fire, and walk out, giving such a slap o' the door that the boy thought the house couldn't help tumbling down.

Well, to be sure, if there wasn't a hullabulloo next morning, when the poor fellow told his story! They could talk of nothing else the whole day. One said one thing, another said another, but a fat, lazy scullery girl said the wittiest thing of all. 'Musha!' says she, 'if the pooka does be cleaning up every-thing that way when we're asleep, what should we be slaving ourselves for, doing his work?' '*Sha gu dheine*,' says another, 'them's the wisest words you ever said, Cauth: it's meself won't contradict you.'

84

So said so done. Not a bit of a plate or dish saw a drop of water that evening, and not a besom was laid on the floor, and every one went to bed soon after sundown. Next morning everything was as fine as fire in the kitchen, and the lord mayor might eat his dinner off the flags. It was great ease to the lazy servants, you may depend, and everything went on well till a foolhardy gag of a boy said he would stay up one night and have a chat with the pooka.

He was a little daunted when the door was thrown open, and the ass marched up to the fire. He didn't open his mouth till the pot was filled, and the pooka lying snug and sausty before the fire.

'Ah then, sir!', says he, at last, picking up courage, 'if it isn't taking a liberty, might I ax who you are, and why are you so kind as to do half of the day's work for the girls every night?' 'No liberty at all,' says the pooka, says he, 'I'll tell you, and welcome. I was a servant here in the time of Squire R.'s father, and was the laziest rogue that ever was clothed and fed, and done nothing for it. When my time came for the other world, this is the punishment was laid on me—to come here, and do all this labour every night, and then go out in the cold. It isn't so bad in the fine weather, but if you only knew what it is to stand with your head between your legs, facing the storm, from midnight to sunrise on a bleak winter night!' 'And could we do anything for your comfort, my poor fellow?' says the boy. 'Musha, I don't know,' says the pooka, 'but I think a good quilted frieze coat would help to keep the life in me, them long nights.' 'Why then, in troth, we'd be the ungratefulest of people if we didn't feel for you.'

To make a long story short, the next night but two the boy was there again; and if he didn't delight the poor pooka, holding up a fine warm coat before him, it's no matter! Betune the pooka and the man, his legs were got into the four arms of it, and it was buttoned down his breast and his belly, and he was so pleased he walked up to the glass to see how he looked. 'Well,' says he, 'it's a long lane that has no turning. I am much obliged to yourself and your fellow-servants. Yous have made me happy at last. Good-night to you.'

So he was walking out, but the other cried, 'Och! sure you're going too soon. What about the washing and sweeping?' 'Ah, you may tell the girls that they must now get their turn. My punishment was to last till I was thought worthy of a reward for the way I done my duty. You'll see me no more.' And no more they did, and right sorry they were for being in such a hurry to reward the ungrateful pooka.

27: THE KILDARE LURIKEEN

A young girl that lived in sight of Castle Carberry, near Edenderry, was going for a pitcher of
water to the neighbouring well one summer morning, when who should she see sitting in a sheltery
nook under an old thorn, but the Lurikeen, work-
ing like vengeance at a little old brogue only fit for
the foot of a fairy like himself. There he was,
boring his holes, and jerking his waxed ends, with
his little three-cornered hat with gold lace, his
knee-breeches, his jug of beer by his side, and his
pipe in his mouth. He was so busy at his work, and
so taken up with an old ballad he was singing in
Irish, that he did not mind Bridget till she had him
by the scruff o' the neck, as if he was in a vice. 'Ah,
what are you doin'?' says he, turning his head
round as well as he could. 'Dear, dear! To think of
such a purty colleen ketchin' a body, as if he was
after robbin' a hen roost! What did I do to be
trated in such an undecent manner? The very vul-
garest young ruffin in the townland could do no
worse. Come, come, Miss Bridget, take your hands
off, sit down, and us have a chat, like two respec-
table people.' 'Ah, Mr Lurikeen, I don't care a wisp
of *borrach* for your politeness. It's your money I
want, and I won't take hand or eye from you till
you put me in possession of a fine lob of it.'
'Money, indeed! Ah! Where would a poor cobbler
like me get it? Anyhow there's no money here-
abouts, and if you'll only let go my arms, I'll turn

my pockets inside out, and open the drawer of my seat, and give you leave to keep every halfpenny you'll find.' 'That won't do. My eye'll keep going through you like darning needles till I have the gold. Begonies, if you don't make haste, I'll carry you, head and pluck, into the village, and there you'll have thirty pair of eyes on you instead of one.' 'Well, well, was ever a poor cobbler so circumvented! And if it was an ignorant, ugly bosthoon that done it, I would not wonder, but a decent, comely girl, that can read her *Poor Man's Manual* at the chapel, and——' 'You may throw your compliments on the stream there; they won't do for me, I tell you. The gold, the gold, the gold! Don't take up my time with your blarney.' 'Well, if there's any to be got, it's under the ould castle it is; we must have a walk for it. Just put me down and we'll get on.' 'Put you down indeed! I know a trick worth two of that; I'll carry you.' 'Well, how suspicious we are! Do you see the castle from this?' Bridget was about turning her eyes from the little man to where she knew the castle stood, but she bethought herself in time.

They went up a little hill-side, and the Lurikeen was quite reconciled, and laughed and joked. But just as they got to the brow, he looked up over the ditch, gave a great screech, and shouted just as if a bugle horn was blew at her ears. 'Oh, murdher! Castle Carberry is afire.' Poor Bridget gave a great start, and looked towards the castle. The same moment she missed the weight of the Lurikeen, and when her eyes fell where he was a moment before, there was no more sign of him than if everything that passed was a dream.

GLOSSARY

For the benefit of the readers unfamiliar with the Irish language this list of Irish words (or words derived from Irish) is appended. In translating we have endeavoured not only to give verbal equivalences but also to convey something of the flavour of the meaning of the original Irish.

Angashore *(ainniseoir)* — wretch
Bean Sighe — female fairy
Ben-a-teagh *(bean an tí)* — housewife, woman of
                                                    the house
Birreds *(bairéad)* — beret
Bochyeen *(bualtrach)* — dried cow dung
Bodach — an Irish term of great contempt
Boolian buí — rag weed
Cappeen dearg *(caipín dearg)* — red cap
Clann Sighe — fairy family
Cruith — hump
Daoine Matha *(Daoine Maithe)* — fairies
Deck — pack
Deeg *(gíog)* — a squeek
Dhrass — bout (bout of crying)
Duine Sighe — fairy people
Fir Dhorocha — dark man
Greeshach *(gríosach)* — embers
Knoc *(cnoc)* — hill
Lewd — ashamed
Lussmore — fox-glove (fairy finger)

Misnach — courage

Ounkran — cross creature

Omadhan *(amadán)* — fool

Onshuch *(Óinseach)* — female fool

Ovoch *(A mhac)* — son

Phoca — seal

Piast — sea-serpent

Pishrogues — witchcraft or superstitious practices

Puckeen — football

Sha gu dhuine *(sea go deimhin)* — Yes, certainly

Sheeoge — fairy

Shemus Rua — Red James

Shone Feol — I want meat

Sthronshuch — untidy negligent girl

Stim — whit (particle)

Thruckeen *(tuicín)* — young girl

Vanithee *(bean an tí)* — housewife, woman of the house

Vuaya *(vuya)* — another form of Mhuire, Mary (Blessed Virgin)

FOLKTALES OF THE IRISH COUNTRYSIDE
Kevin Danaher

In this heartwarming collection of tales that
spring naturally from the Irish countryside, Kevin
Danaher remembers some forty stories told to him
long ago when country folk entertained themselves
of an evening with singing, dancing and
storytelling. Some are stories told by members of
his own family; others he took down in his own
countryside from the last of the great traditional
seanchaí. Included are tales of giants and ghosts,
of wondrous deeds and queer happenings, of fairies
and kings, beautiful princesses and wicked
mischief-makers.

IRISH FIRESIDE FOLKTALES
Patrick Kennedy

The fireside stories of the Irish people are part of a heritage unparalleled in the oral literature of the world. Certainly, no other nation has preserved by word of mouth such an exuberance of riddles, sayings, curses, blessings, prayers and ballads. Nowhere has the art of story-telling been more richly developed than in Ireland: through the centuries generations of story-tellers have handed down folktales of all kinds. At a time when modern life had not yet spread into the remotest corners of the countryside, story-telling was a favourite entertainment in the quietness of long country evenings. The voices of Seanchaí and wise woman, of wandering pedlar or spalpeen, gathered the people round the fireside and audiences listened to legends and anecdotes, religious, heroic and romantic tales.

Colourful, vivid, whimiscal, these stories bring alive the fireside scene of bygone days. Everything is told as if it happened to the story-teller himself, and as if these extraordinary events could happen to you or anybody.

IRISH LIFE AND LORE
Séamas Ó Catháin

Irish Life and Lore is not only an excellent collection of folktales and legends but it is also packed with the lore and traditions of places and people from the four corners of Ireland.

This book contains much new material which was never published before and which is drawn from the manuscript archive of the former Irish Folklore commission, now the Department of Irish Folklore at University College, Dublin and also from the living Irish folk tradition of today.

Irish Life and Lore includes authentic folk material culled from nineteenth century writers such as Kennedy and Crofton Croker and also from the author's own extensive field collections made in various parts of the country.

THE BEDSIDE BOOK OF IRISH FOLKLORE
Séamas Ó Catháin

The Bedside Book of Irish Folklore is crammed with colourful folktales and legends, tales of the ghost and fairy world and traditional customs and beliefs which were and are an important part of Irish life.

Here you can find riddles and proverbs and tall tales galore. You will also discover cures and remedies for all types of ailments: from baldness to drunkenness and even advice on love potions.

These stories, gathered from the four corners of Ireland, are told in the original words of the storytellers and make lively and exciting reading.

BOOK OF IRISH CURSES

Patrick C. Power

Cursing is generally understood to mean the use of certain earthy expressions and also the light-hearted picturesque language which sometimes derives from formal cursing. In this book the nature and reality of formal cursing is explored. An attempt is made to answer the questions: Can one bring misfortune on another by expressing the wish formally? Has it ever been done?

A remarkable blend of history, folklore, and anecdote, this is above all a book about people and about cursing as an ancient and mysterious agency of their fears and hatreds. In the most evocative and telling part of the book Dr Power discusses the Priest's Curse and the Widow's Curse. The curse of the 'broken priest' in particular had a singular and malevolent power; and, even today, the words of a sober general practitioner in a country town linger uncomfortably in the mind: 'Keep in with the priests! It is not lucky to fall out with them!' The Widow's Curse was the most deadly of all. Her very helplessness gave her imprecations a strange force of their own. She would kneel and loosen her hair as she solemnly cursed those who had wronged her. To read of the Widow's Curse is to be aware, if only for a moment, of the great night-world that surrounds the tiny lighted arena we call 'reality'.

SUPERSTITIONS OF THE IRISH COUNTRY PEOPLE
Padraic O'Farrell

Do you know why it is considered unlucky

- to meet a barefooted man?
- to start out on a journey on 10th November?
- to get married on a Saturday?

Irish country people believed that fairies were always present among them and that around the next corner or in the very next clump of thistles there might well be somebody lurking who would lead them to the crock of gold at the end of the rainbow. Fairies were good to mortals who observed the superstitions which called for leaving them food, not throwing out water without first shouting a warning to them, and so on. They even parted with some of their golden apples, waters of wisdom and swords of knowledge to such considerate people.

A cairn of fascinating lore is contained in the pages of this book — ancient customs relating to spirits and fairies, sea and water, milk and food, plants and cures, weather, animals, love, marriage and death.

GEMS OF IRISH WISDOM: IRISH PROVERBS AND SAYINGS
Padraic O'Farrel

Gems of Irish Wisdom is a fascinating collection of Irish proverbs and sayings.

The tallest flowers hide the strongest nettles.
The man who asks what good is money has already paid for his plot.
A man begins cutting his wisdom teeth the first time he bites off more than he can chew.
Even if you are on the right track, you'll be run over if you stay there.
The road to Heaven is well signposted but badly lit at night.
Love is like stirabout, it must be made fresh every day.
The begrudger is as important a part of Irish life as the muck he throws.
Love at first sight often happens in the twilight.
The man who hugs the altar-rails doesn't always hug his own wife.
If a man fools me once, shame on him. If he fools me twice, shame on me.
God never closes one door but He opens another.
Every cock crows on his own dunghill.
A kind word never gets a man into trouble.